From Darkness to Light

The Memoirs of a Healing Mind

Faustino Lopez, III

Copyright © 2024

2024922799

All Rights Reserved

Dedication

To the infinite universe of yesterday, today, and tomorrow—where time bends and memories collide, where the echoes of our struggles and triumphs drift like constellations across the night sky. May we forever seek the light, no matter how distant it may seem, and may we find solace in the knowledge that every journey, no matter how dark, brings us closer to understanding ourselves and our place in this boundless cosmos.

Acknowledgment

This book is the culmination of countless moments of introspection, perseverance, and the unwavering support of those who stood by me during my darkest hours. My deepest gratitude extends to Headspace, The UTRGV Psychology Clinic, Infinite Love Meditation Center, and Healing Minds Counseling. Through their guidance, I was given the tools to navigate a complex labyrinth of emotions, finding solace in a journey toward healing. To my friends, colleagues, and family, who offered their patience and understanding when I was at my most vulnerable—thank you for being my anchors when the storm raged fiercest. And to the individuals whose stories became entwined with my own over the years, I acknowledge your pain and strength; your struggles were the mirror that helped me see my own. This book is a testament to all of you, and without your presence in my life, it would not exist.

Contents

Dedication iv

Acknowledgment v

Comfortably Numb 1

Friendships 3

Heaven, Hell, You, and I 5

My Eternal Apology 7

Last Root 10

High on the Hollow 12

Elegy of a Nation 14

Echoes in the Silence 16

Echoes in the Abyss 18

Echoes in the Void 21

Echoes of Our Chains 24

My Reflection 26

In the Shade of Kindness 28

Forged in the Shadows 30

Echoes of the Living Grave 33

Echoes of the Clock 35

Echoes in the Dark	37
A Kindness Returned	40
Forward's Flame	42
Echoes of the Open Road	44
Dad	46
A Rebellion of Shadows	48
The Roots We Bear	51
Kindred Fires	53
Ripples of Infinity	55
In the Quiet Now	57
Embers in the Dark	59
Eternity in a Moment	62
Eternity's Edge	63
The Dawn Within	65
Horizons Unseen	68
Forge of the Moment	72
In the Shadow's Embrace	75
Inner Sanctum	77
Ironclad	79

Serene Madness	82
The Echo of Resistance	84
The Gaze of Death	87
The Keeper's Mind	89
The Quiet of Knowing	91
The Solitary Sentinel	93
The Tapestry of Us	95
The Threshold of Unknowing	97
The Unyielding	99
Thread of Souls	101
Threads of Becoming	103
Three Lives Lived	105
To My Loving Parents	107
Unveiling the Mirror	109
Unveiling the Serpent	111
Unyielding Flame	114
Unyielding Flame -2	116
Whispers in the Abyss	119
Ephemeral Echoes	122

The Pillar of Solitude 124

Democracy 2024 126

The Art of Release 128

The Churn 130

Beacon Within 133

Echoes of Grace 135

In Defiance of the Dark.. 137

My Legacy 139

About The Author 141

From Darkness to Light

Comfortably Numb

In a world that trembles, ever-shifting,

Where nothing holds, and tides are always drifting,

I've found my solace, my steady tide,

In a numbness deep, where emotions reside.

Comfortably numb, I stand apart,

Shielding the chambers of my fragile heart.

Tragedy and joy, sorrow's keen sting,

Cannot touch me, in the cocoon I cling.

For in this tempest of life's grand play,

Numbness is my anchor, keeping storms at bay.

With every gust and turn of the dice,

I remain unswayed, cold as ice.

My mastery of feelings, a strength indeed,

Protects my soul, fulfills every need.

Faustino Lopez, III

Yet behind this fortress, so tall and wide,

Lies a realm untouched, feelings I hide.

For no one knows, no one can see,

The tempest of emotions raging in me.

Expressionless, my face remains still,

But deep inside, passions are never still.

In the sanctuary of numbness, I've found my peace,

Yet the cost I've paid, it does not cease.

For to be untouched by life's ebb and flow,

Is to miss the depth of emotions that grow.

From Darkness to Light

Friendships

In a world where screens light up the night,

Where every facade is a digital sight,

I stand on the edge, looking within,

Keeping a distance, preserving my skin.

Just a few souls know the depth of my core,

A handful of friends, not one person more.

Professional ties, acquaintances fleet,

Connections that end once their purpose is neat.

The digital realm with its shimmer and sheen,

It hides what's beneath, what's rarely seen.

For in its vast echo, where truths often bend,

Nothing is real, nor the likes that it sends.

Don't offer me hearts from a faceless array,

I've no care for the hollow play.

Faustino Lopez, III

Genuine warmth, not the digital trend,

It is the currency I spend with a friend.

Trust isn't granted by mere association,

It's a long journey, filled with observation.

For once it is broken, its pieces turn to sand,

You're etched in the tome of the forever damned.

In this crowded expanse, where masks often slide,

My sanctuary is privacy, where truths reside.

In a world where pretense is the ultimate art,

I guard my soul, I protect my heart.

From Darkness to Light

Heaven, Hell, You, and I

A tale of eternal life to describe,

A journey beyond the physical realm,

Where souls roam free without a helm.

Heaven, a place of eternal bliss,

Where angels sing, and love exists,

A paradise of peace and light,

Where darkness fades and the day is bright.

But is this truly what you seek?

An endless existence that never grows weak?

A life without pain or strife,

Is it worth the sacrifice of life?

And then there's Hell, a place of fear,

A realm of darkness, death, and tears,

A fiery pit where demons dwell,

Where the damned are sentenced to eternal Hell.

Faustino Lopez, III

But maybe, just maybe, Hell is where I'll thrive,

Where my soul will dance and come alive,

Where pain and suffering fuel my fire,

And darkness becomes my heart's desire.

Eternal life, a blessing or a curse?

A never-ending journey that only gets worse,

For what is life without an end?

A journey that goes on without a friend.

So, Heaven or Hell, which will it be?

A life of peace or agony?

It's up to you, my dear friend,

To choose your path and journey to the end.

From Darkness to Light

My Eternal Apology

In silent chambers of my heart, where whispers dwell,

A barrenness resides, where no spring can swell.

To thee, my compass and my shoreward light,

I pen these words, through the mute of night.

My dearest love, whose warmth exceeds the sun,

Forgive the void in me, the undone that can't be won.

For in the cradle of my soul, where life should sing,

Lies an echo hollow, a faltering wing.

No seed within me breathes, no bloom will grow,

A secret frost, a tide that ebbs but won't flow.

The laughter of a child, the patter of small feet,

Are gardens in a book I shall not meet?

With each talk of babies, my spirit cloaks in thorns,

A wall erected high, a heart that mourns.

Faustino Lopez, III

Though the arms of others may cradle dreams, brand new,

Adoption's gift, my love, is a mirror of my rue.

For in those eyes, not sprung from my own life's line,

I'd see a testament to this flaw of mine.

A reminder stark that I, in nature's script,

Am a character flawed, from the main plot slipped.

How do I love a star that's not born from our night?

Would it not bear the shadow of my plight?

This fear, it clutches with a madman's grip,

A jealous guard 'gainst which I dare not slip.

In my fortress of solitude, in this expanse of fear,

I've locked away the hope of the patter we might hear.

For if I loved a child, not of my flesh, not of my bone,

Would I not resent the seed that I have not sown?

Yet, in your eyes, my only solace and my creed,

From Darkness to Light

I beg for pardon, for this failing of my seed.

A hopelessness grips, an apology I strew,

I'm sorry, my love, for the life I can't give you.

Forgive me for the silence where laughter should be,

For the empty spaces where you dreamt of three.

I stand before you, less than whole, a half not full,

In the echoing void of an empty cradle's pull.

Love's tapestry, we weave with threads fine and small,

I pray thee find it in you to forgive my withdrawal.

And in the quiet of our nights, just us two,

Remember the love, which, though flawed, remains true.

Faustino Lopez, III

Last Root

From the hills of Andalucía, where our name first took flight,

Through centuries, we've wandered, shadows etched in twilight.

My blood sings of ancestors, strong and proud,

But now the echoes falter, beneath this heavy shroud.

In 1480, the tree took root, in fertile Andalusian clay,

Generations carved in stone, enduring night and day.

But here I stand, the final branch, with withered leaves to show,

A barren soul, the fruitless end, where no new seeds will grow.

My father's hands once held the weight of all that came before,

Now cold in death, they pass the torch, yet I can bear no more.

This lineage, once so fierce and bright, now dims and fades away,

For in my chest, a sterile heart, that beats but will not stay.

The burden rests upon my brow, a tombstone yet unwritten,

A silent scream, the final page, where all our tales are smitten.

From Darkness to Light

No child will hear the stories told, no heir to carry on,

This is the end, the last of me—when morning breaks, I'm gone.

So lay me down in quiet earth, where roots have long since spread,

And let the winds of time erase the path where I have tread.

For though I bear this heavy weight, I know the end must be—

The end of all that once was us, the end that rests in me.

Faustino Lopez, III

High on the Hollow

In the quiet night, where shadows bend,

I find my refuge, a fleeting friend,

A bottle, a spark, a fleeting high,

To numb the echoes of a shattered sky.

I chase the moon in a haze of smoke,

Every drag, every sip, another cloak,

Wrapping my heart in layers thin,

Yet the cold of truth still seeps within.

The pain, it lingers, a ghost in the room,

No matter the pleasure, no matter the bloom,

I climb the peaks of momentary bliss,

Only to fall to the depths I miss.

Distractions call with a siren's song,

But the tune, it fades, it doesn't last long,

From Darkness to Light

The night grows old, and the dawn is near,

Bringing with it the same old fear.

I dance on the edge of oblivion's grace,

Trying to outrun the past I face,

But every high brings a deeper low,

A cycle of hurt that continues to grow.

In the end, I'm left with the hollow inside,

The pain I buried, I can't deny,

I walk the path of avoidance and flight,

But the darkness returns with the morning light.

Faustino Lopez, III

Elegy of a Nation

In the stillness of dawn, the mourning begins,

A nation's heart is weighed down by its sins.

Another life, another shattered dream,

Innocence lost in a violent stream.

Crimson echoes in a land of despair,

Where bullets tear through the fragile air.

The old, the young, none spared the grief,

As fear becomes the only belief.

Prayers whispered into the void of night,

Yet no power to turn wrong into right.

Leaders bicker, their words turn to dust,

While the cycle repeats, betraying our trust.

Why can't we live in a harmony sweet?

Why must blood taint every street?

From Darkness to Light

The rivers run red, the sorrow grows,

As the next tragedy strikes its cruel blows.

We seek answers in the shadows of pain,

But they slip through our fingers like the rain.

Another day, another sorrow deep,

As we wonder when our souls will sleep.

Death's cold hand seems always near,

A relentless shadow we all must fear.

Faustino Lopez, III

Echoes in the Silence

In the quiet of the night, shadows start to weep,

For the ghosts of yesteryear, memories I keep.

Every choice a blade, carving through my soul,

Leaving scars that deepen, as the years unroll.

The echoes of my footsteps, on paths I cannot change,

Resound within this hollow heart, a tune so cold, so strange.

Regret's a heavy shroud, draped across my chest,

A burden I carry, denying peaceful rest.

The faces of the past, they haunt my waking dreams,

Whispering of moments lost and fractured, silent screams.

Each mistake a specter, relentless in its chase,

A mirror to my conscience, reflecting every trace.

Pain's a silent partner, walking by my side,

In the labyrinth of memory, there's nowhere left to hide.

From Darkness to Light

Choices like a river flowing through my veins,

Feeding every sorrow, nurturing the pains.

Yet in this endless night, where suffering holds sway,

I search the darkened corners for a glimmer of the day.

But all I find are shadows, reminders of the cost,

Of living with the echoes of every battle lost.

So here I stand, a figure carved from grief,

Haunted by the echoes and yearning for relief.

But in the silence, deep and vast, I find no peace, no light,

Only the weight of choices made, in the long, unyielding night.

Faustino Lopez, III

Echoes in the Abyss

In the quiet of the night, I hear them call,

The whispers of demons, relentless and small,

They rise from the shadows, a siren's sweet song,

Tugging at threads where I know I don't belong.

My veins pulse with fire, a hunger so deep,

A gnawing, a craving that steals away sleep,

Each moment, a battle, a war in my soul,

The desire to break free, yet losing control.

I've danced with the darkness, surrendered to vice,

Paid for my choices, the ultimate price,

In mirrors, I see the hollowed-out eyes,

A reflection of lies, of failures, of sighs.

The bottle, the needle, the pills I have kissed,

Promised relief in their poisonous mist,

From Darkness to Light

But the comfort they bring is fleeting at best,

Leaving me hollow, a ghost, and the rest.

Regret is a shackle, a weight on my chest,

A constant reminder that I am not blessed,

Yet somewhere within, a flicker of light,

A yearning for change, to fight through the night.

I claw at the surface, I struggle, I strain,

Desperate to rise from this cycle of pain,

But the demons, they linger, they never let go,

A part of my being, as deep as my woe.

Is there a way out, a path to be free?

Or am I condemned to this endless decree?

I seek out the meaning, the reason, the why,

Yet answers evade me as days drift on by.

Oh, to be new, to shed this old skin,

Faustino Lopez, III

To start fresh again, to find peace within,

But the battle rages on, both in heart and in mind,

In the echoes of the abyss, true meaning I'll find.

But for now, I linger in this fragile state,

Between hope and despair, between love and hate,

And though I may stumble, may falter, may fall,

I'll rise once again, answering the call.

From Darkness to Light

Echoes in the Void

In the quiet hours before the dawn,

Where shadows stretch, but no light is born,

I walk a path of wandering thought,

In search of meaning, though meaning's caught—

Somewhere beyond the veil of mind,

Where questions echo, undefined.

Is there purpose in the steps I take,

Or just the noise that ripples lakes?

Each breath I draw, a silent plea,

For answers that elude, that flee—

Into the depths of doubt and fear,

Where certainty is never near.

What am I but dust and dream,

A fleeting flicker in a stream?

Of consciousness, a fragile flame,

Faustino Lopez, III

That flickers with a nameless name—

In the vast expanse of endless night,

I seek the dawn, the smallest light.

Emotions churn like restless seas,

Tides of sorrow, waves of ease,

Yet, in their flow, no anchor found,

Just endless drifting, round and round—

A sailor lost without a star,

In search of who and what we are.

And so I ponder, day and night,

In deep shadows, in blinding light,

The why, the how, the if, the when,

The paths that lead to where and when—

Yet all I find is what I lose,

In the silence, where the echoes choose.

To leave me here, in doubt's embrace,

From Darkness to Light

A traveler with no set place,

But still, I walk, and still I try,

To catch the whispers of the sky—

To understand, to simply be,

In this endless search for me.

Faustino Lopez, III

Echoes of Our Chains

In the quiet dawn, we whisper dreams,

Of joy unbound, where the soul redeems,

Yet, in the shadows of each waking day,

We tread the path we've sworn to stray.

We speak of freedom, unchained and wild,

Yet cling to the comforts that beguile,

We plant the seeds of our own despair,

In gardens tended with utmost care.

The mirror reflects what we refuse to see,

The hands that bind us, are ours, not free,

We dance in circles, our shackles tight,

Cursing the darkness, while fearing the light.

For every cry of joy, we seek,

We echo pain in words we speak,

From Darkness to Light

Repeating woes in a siren's call,

Building walls where we long to fall.

So here we stand, at the crossroads' edge,

With keys in hand, yet bound by pledge,

To chains, we forged with wishes bold,

In pursuit of happiness, we grip the cold.

If freedom we desire, truly so,

Why then do we let our burdens grow?

In every choice, a path is lain,

To break the cycle, to shatter the chain.

Faustino Lopez, III

My Reflection

In the throes of anguish, my will took shape,

A silent forge where my strength was made.

Amid the tumult, chaos vast and wild,

Came lessons of stillness, soft and mild.

In the grip of fear, where shadows loom,

I found the might that in me bloomed.

It was in the deepest dark I faced,

That flickering light, my path was traced.

Thus, pain became the ground, firm and true,

Where from the earth, my courage grew.

Chaos taught my heart to rest, to see,

In the eye of the storm, tranquility.

Fear, the harsh mentor, stern and wise,

Revealed the power that in me lies.

From Darkness to Light

And in the darkest night, my soul's bright flare,

Showed the way out, from despair's snare.

For only through trials we truly find,

The full expanse of the heart and mind.

Only by facing night do we know,

The truest light in us does glow.

Faustino Lopez, III

In the Shade of Kindness

I don't often seek the company of strangers,

But today was different, in an unexpected way.

In the slow line for fast food, a never-ending wait,

I noticed a man and his dog beneath a tree,

Seeking shade from the unforgiving South Texas sun.

This man, I thought, is someone I'd like to meet.

As minutes dragged on, I saw another pause,

To offer spare change and exchange a few words,

A prayer shared in passing, then each went on their way.

Still, I stood in line, the wait seeming endless.

Finally, my order was called, and I hurried over,

Drawn to that tree where the man and his dog sat.

He told me his name was Maximiliano, his companion, Dennis.

I handed him a burger, fries, and a drink,

And with a grateful smile, he said, "Thank you."

From Darkness to Light

Then, just as quietly as we'd met, we parted,

Each to continue our separate journeys under the same sun.

Faustino Lopez, III

Forged in the Shadows

In the twilight, where light meets dark,

A soul stands firm, though bruised and scarred,

The weight of night, it pulls, it strains,

Yet onward steps, despite the chains.

Temptation whispers, soft and low,

"Relinquish hope, let courage go."

But in the heart, a fire burns bright,

A spark that flares against the night.

The path is steep, with thorns and snare,

A journey made in doubt and prayer,

Yet every fall, each bitter taste,

Feeds a will too strong to waste.

In shadows deep, where demons tread,

The echoes of the fallen dead,

From Darkness to Light

A vow is made, with breath so cold,

To carve a future, fierce and bold.

For in this dance of dark and light,

Both sin and virtue claim their right,

To mold a life, to shape a man,

Forged in the fire of fate's cruel hand.

Though tempests rage, and sirens call,

This heart will stand, it will not fall,

For even in the darkest hour,

Resilience blooms, a stubborn flower.

No saintly path, nor purest way,

But one where shadows blend with day,

Where every choice, both wrong and right,

Builds a destiny, fought in the night.

So onward strides this weary soul,

Faustino Lopez, III

With eyes fixed on the distant goal,

For in the struggle, fierce and long,

Is found the strength to carry on.

And though the scars will never fade,

They mark the path where courage played,

In every wound, a story told,

Of battles fought, of spirits bold.

For life's true victory is won,

Not by the sinless, but by the one

Who rises, falls, and rises still,

With iron heart, and iron will.

From Darkness to Light

Echoes of the Living Grave

In silent halls where shadows tread,

We bury dreams, though we're not dead.

The clock's cold tick, a whispered knell,

Reminds us all, we weave our hell.

Once, fires burned with fierce delight,

But now, they smolder out of sight.

The heart that danced in youthful flame,

Now aches with time, a ghosted name.

What dies within, no eyes can see,

A subtle theft of what we'd be.

Ambitions wilt, their roots now bare,

A grave within, none else aware.

For it's not death that robs us most,

But living life as empty hosts.

Faustino Lopez, III

The greatest loss, the quiet fade,

Of all the selves we never made.

So heed the whisper in the night,

Revive the spark, reclaim the fight.

For while we breathe, the chance remains,

To break these self-imposed chains.

Memento mori, the truth is clear,

But what lives within, we must hold dear.

For though the body meets its end,

The soul's decay is what we must mend.

In every breath, a choice is cast,

To live anew or mourn the past.

For life is brief, but worse, we find,

Is dying slowly in the mind.

From Darkness to Light

Echoes of the Clock

In shadows long and deep, the minutes crawl,
An endless stretch of days, we barely heed,
Each moment whispers softly, but we stall,
Till time, unbidden, overtakes our speed.

The youthful dawn we chased with eager feet,
Now slips unnoticed, lost in twilight's haze,
What once was vibrant fades, now bittersweet,
As age creeps in, erasing summer's blaze.

We chase the sun, but find the night instead,
The plans we spun unravel, thread by thread,
For time, indifferent, marches on ahead,
And leaves behind the words we left unsaid.

So seize the day, before it slips away,
For time's cold hand will not delay its claim,

Faustino Lopez, III

In every fleeting hour, a life we pay,

The echo of the clock, our hearts' refrain.

Yet still we dream, with hope against the tide,

Though time may steal, it cannot break our stride.

From Darkness to Light

Echoes in the Dark

In the mirror's silent gaze, I find,

A face that shifts, unravels, and rewinds.

The lines once firm, now blurred and grey,

Time's fingers trace where youth decayed.

Who am I, beneath this shifting skin?

A stranger's voice speaks deep within.

Echoes of a life once known,

Now fractured, lost, and overthrown.

In the shadows of my former self, I tread,

Through corridors of doubt and dread.

Each step a question, each breath a sigh,

As I wrestle with the reasons why.

The clock ticks on, indifferent, cold,

As I search for truth in stories old.

Faustino Lopez, III

But truth eludes, a wraith in flight,

Dancing just beyond my sight.

What is this change that rends my soul?

Is it a loss or some forgotten goal?

A metamorphosis, or a slow decay,

Or merely time's relentless play?

In this abyss, I stand alone,

A soul unmoored, a heart of stone.

Yet in the depths, a spark still burns,

A flicker of the self that yearns—

To understand, to grasp, to hold,

The essence of a life retold.

And though the answers may not come,

I walk this path, I won't succumb.

For in the struggle, there is light,

From Darkness to Light

A fragile hope that dims the night.

And as I change, I come to see,

The self I seek is born in me.

Faustino Lopez, III

A Kindness Returned

Through the years, I've sown small seeds of grace,

Not as a saint, but simply human, flawed,

With deeds that try to balance out the weight

Of all my sins, though knowing they're not enough

To open Heaven's gates for one like me.

One day, amid the rush of daily life,

I stopped to grab a meal—a fleeting pause—

But as I reached to pay, my heart sank fast;

I'd left my wallet at home, and there I stood,

Empty-handed, feeling small and lost.

Yet, when I met the eyes behind the glass,

A warm smile greeted me, and with a nod,

She handed me my meal, waved me away.

I promised to return, to make things right—

But she just smiled, "No worries, it's on me."

From Darkness to Light

Half an hour later, back I went,

Insisting on the payment I'd forgot,

But still, she wouldn't take a single cent.

Her kindness shone as bright as morning sun,

And I drove off, my spirit lifted high.

It struck me then—a twist of fate, perhaps—

That in this simple act, a lesson lay:

Today, the world had turned and shown me grace,

And for a fleeting moment, I dared dream

That she might be the one to guard Heaven's gates.

Though unworthy, I was full and glad,

Content with this small blessing life had sent.

Faustino Lopez, III

Forward's Flame

Forward's Flame ignites the dawn,

Where shadows of the past are gone.

The path ahead, with steps untraced,

Holds more than what was left in haste.

The echoes of what once has been,

Are whispers lost upon the wind.

Yet in the light of what's to come,

The heart beats stronger, not undone.

For life is not a backward glance,

Nor tethered by a bygone dance.

The future sings a brighter tune,

Beneath the endless, rising moon.

So cast your eyes where dreams reside,

And let the past drift with the tide.

From Darkness to Light

The life before you, bold and true,

Is where your soul finds something new.

In every breath, the promise gleams,

That forward lies the truest dreams.

So walk with purpose, steady stride,

For life ahead shall be your guide.

Faustino Lopez, III

Echoes of the Open Road

In the quiet hush of morning's breath,

Where the horizon meets the sky,

I chose the path with untamed steps,

Not the things that money buys.

I gathered memories like fallen leaves,

Each one a story softly told,

Not trinkets bound to gather dust,

But tales that never grow old.

The wind it whispered through the trees,

Of lands I'd yet to see,

Of mountains high and rivers deep,

Of where my heart could truly be.

I filled my days with laughter's songs,

And nights with skies aglow,

For in the wild embrace of life,

From Darkness to Light

There's more than riches show.

So let the world have golden things,

And houses filled with stone,

I'll take the stars, the endless road,

And stories to call my own.

For when the years have settled in,

And silver crowns my hair,

It's the echoes of adventures past,

That will linger in the air.

And when they ask what did you own,

What treasures did you find?

I'll smile and say, "I lived my life,

With stories etched in time."

Faustino Lopez, III

Dad

In the quiet moments of dawn's embrace,

I remember you, Father, your enduring grace.

Your steady hands and heart so wide,

Were the pillars where we could always confide.

You were the beacon, guiding our way,

Encouraging dreams, come what may.

In your eyes, we saw the fire,

That fueled our hearts and lifted us higher.

From life's first breath to every endeavor,

Your love was a constant, unwavering, forever.

You taught us to dream, to reach for the skies,

To find our own path and never compromise.

Now you've joined those who've gone before,

In the realm where spirits soar.

With your parents, in that tranquil place,

From Darkness to Light

I envision you, wrapped in eternal grace.

We know life's journey is a fleeting dance,
Each step a chance, a cosmic trance.
One day, I'll join you, in that boundless domain,
Where souls are free, beyond earthly pain.

Until then, I'll cherish the infinite gifts,
The love that through time, never drifts.
In the vast universe, your presence lingers,
In the touch of the wind, the warmth of the sun's fingers.

Thank you, Father, for always being there,
For the love, the wisdom, the endless care.
Your legacy lives on, in every dream we pursue,
In the infinite blessings, in the memory of you.

Faustino Lopez, III

A Rebellion of Shadows

In the silence of night, where whispers convene,

I stand on the edge of the world's unseen,

A figure cast in shades of gray,

Questioning the light of day.

Who am I, if not this storm?

A soul unraveled, yet reborn.

I wear the scars of battles past,

In every wound, a truth is cast.

The universe, a cold expanse,

Reflects my gaze, a searching trance.

Am I a fragment, lost in the void?

Or the architect of all destroyed?

I grapple with the ties that bind,

The chains that fetter heart and mind,

From Darkness to Light

But in this struggle, I arise,

A rebel against the countless lies.

I've sought in stars, in endless skies,

The meaning is veiled by endless whys.

Yet, in my core, a fire burns,

A force that, through the darkness churns.

I defy the shadows, I defy the pain,

In every loss, there's much to gain.

The self I seek is forged in strife,

A mosaic of a fractured life.

In every tear, a diamond shines,

In every fall, a strength refines.

I am the tempest, I am the flame,

No longer lost to the cosmic game.

With every breath, I claim my right,

Faustino Lopez, III

To exist in both the day and night.

For in this paradox, I find,

A truth that resonates with time.

I am both nothing and all there is,

A wanderer in an abyss,

But in my depths, I see the dawn,

And from the shadows, I am drawn.

Resilient, whole, defiant, free,

In my reflection, I finally see,

That is the struggle, I have grown,

And in this journey, I've found my own.

A rebellion of shadows, a dance with fate,

In the search for self, I cultivate,

A universe within, vast and deep,

Where the soul, at last, can cease to weep.

From Darkness to Light

The Roots We Bear

To love this skin, this bone, this scar,

You must embrace the roads you've crossed,

The nights you broke, the battles lost,

The echoes deep that left you marred.

For every tear that fell like rain,

Each wound that bled, each whispered lie,

Are threads that weave the reasons why

You stand today, defying pain.

The shadows long, the dreams once torn,

They carved you into something fierce,

And through the dark, despite the fears,

You found a way to be reborn.

So let your past, with all its weight,

Be not a chain, but roots that grow.

Faustino Lopez, III

For even thorns have taught you so—

To love yourself, you can't berate.

The steps you took, the scars you wore,

They're not mistakes, but tales to tell.

A journey through your private hell,

That shaped you into something more.

To love who stands before the glass,

You must forgive the roads you've roamed,

For all you've lost, and all you've owned—

These are the truths that let you last.

From Darkness to Light

Kindred Fires

In the hush between heartbeats, we find our flame,

A spark that flickers in the eyes of those who know,

Who wander the same unmarked path, untamed,

Where dreams intertwine and passions grow.

We gather like whispers in the still of night,

Drawn by a force that words can't bind,

Nurtured by souls who share our sight,

A reflection of spirit, both fierce and kind.

With every step, we kindle the blaze,

Fueling the embers that dare not fade,

Together, we dance through life's wild maze,

A tribe of souls, unafraid, unmade.

For in this circle, we find our grace,

A refuge from the world's endless storm,

Faustino Lopez, III

Where hearts ignite in a sacred space,

And like-minded souls keep each other warm.

So let us burn, with purpose and light,

Bound by a mission, clear and true,

Nurturing souls, we rise to the heights,

In the fire of others, we find our hue.

From Darkness to Light

Ripples of Infinity

In each breath, a wave is born,

Unseen currents, silent storms.

A whisper here, a gesture there,

Shape the world with tender care.

Thoughts like seeds beneath the soil,

Words that weave or threads that spoil.

In every action, vast and small,

We etch our mark upon the wall.

The sky's no limit, nor the sea,

For boundless is our energy.

We are the hands that mold the clay,

To carve the dawn from night's decay.

One spark can light a thousand fires,

One dream can fuel a world's desires.

Faustino Lopez, III

We are the ripples in the stream,

Infinite, boundless, we are the dream.

So let us rise, with purpose clear,

To mend the wounds, to cast out fear.

For in our hearts, the truth does dwell,

That we can change this world as well.

Each step, each word, each silent plea,

A force for change, for all to see.

Our potential, like the stars above,

Is limitless, when born of love.

From Darkness to Light

In the Quiet Now

In the stillness, where the echoes fade,

We find the present, undisturbed by time's parade.

The past, a shadow, no longer clings,

The future, a dream, with silent wings.

Here we sit, where moments gleam,

Not lost in what was, nor what might seem.

The world turns on, its ceaseless dance,

But we remain in quiet trance.

Each breath a gift, each heartbeat true,

The sky above, an endless blue.

No weight of yesterdays, no tomorrows to chase,

Just this moment, a sacred place.

Let the winds of time rush past,

We are here, still, at last.

Faustino Lopez, III

In the quiet now, where peace is found,

We stand unshaken, on holy ground.

From Darkness to Light

Embers in the Dark

In the dead of night, when the world's asleep,

I burn with a fire, fierce and deep.

Frustration's claws, they dig in tight,

But I rise each time, ready to fight.

I've stumbled through shadows, lost my way,

Tripped on the stones that others lay.

Yet in every fall, I've found my stride,

For each bruise and scar, I've never lied.

The sweat on my brow, the ache in my bones,

Whispers of doubt in hollow tones,

They try to break, they try to bind,

But I forge ahead, unyielding in mind.

I'm not the same as I was before,

Each failure's a lesson, opening a door.

Faustino Lopez, III

The nights are long, the road is rough,

But I'm made of grit, and that's enough.

I hammer away at the walls that confine,

With hands that bleed, I carve my sign.

I'll leave my mark, I'll stake my claim,

In the heart of chaos, I'll etch my name.

Through the smoke and ash, I see the light,

A distant spark in the blackest night.

I'm not defeated, I'm not undone,

For the hardest battles are the ones I've won.

So let the world throw what it may,

I'll rise again, come what may.

In every struggle, in every pain,

I find the strength to stand again.

For I am more than flesh and bone,

From Darkness to Light

I am the storm, the breaking stone.

In the depths of night, my spirit's bright,

An ember that refuses to fade from sight.

And though the path is steep and long,

I'll keep on moving, fierce and strong.

For in my heart, there's a burning fire,

A relentless will, a never-tired desire.

I'll break these chains, I'll rise above,

With every step, I'll redefine love.

For in my soul, I know it's true,

The greatest battles bring out the best in you.

Faustino Lopez, III

Eternity in a Moment

Live freely, as though time's endless stream,

Unfolds before us like a golden dream,

With every breath, a promise yet untold,

A journey vast, where we dare to be bold.

Yet, hold each moment close, as if the last,

For life's fleeting whispers fade too fast,

Gratefully, we dance on borrowed time,

Aware the clock could cease its chime.

In the boundless sky of our desires,

We chase the sun, ignite our fires,

But in each shadowed hour, we know,

The fragile threads that life may sew.

So live, my friend, with boundless heart,

Embrace the end, yet never part,

For in this paradox, we find our way,

Eternity wrapped in a single day.

From Darkness to Light

Eternity's Edge

We walk on the edge of forever's light,

With hearts that pulse in endless flight,

Yet shadows loom, dark and near,

Whispering of time, of end, of fear.

To live as though the stars won't fade,

A dream that dances, never swayed,

Yet in each breath, the truth unfolds,

That life is fragile, soft, and cold.

We grasp at joy with open hands,

Knowing well the shifting sands,

That time, unyielding, marches on,

From dusk to dawn, from dusk to dawn.

So let us sing with bold voices,

As though our tale will never grow old,

Faustino Lopez, III

But in our song, a note of grace,

For fleeting moments, we embrace.

To live, to love, without a net,

In endless days, we do forget,

Yet in the night, when silence falls,

Gratitude answers when life calls.

For in this dance on eternity's edge,

We balance fear with hope's pledge,

To live freely, without regret,

And cherish all we can't forget.

From Darkness to Light

The Dawn Within

In the quiet breath before the light,

Where shadows stretch and stars take flight,

A whisper calls from depths unseen,

To wake, to rise, from the dreamer's sheen.

Through veils of sleep where time forgets,

The soul is bound by silent nets,

Yet there, beneath the surface calm,

Awaits the pulse, the ancient psalm.

Remember now the fire's spark,

That flickers still within the dark,

A flame not lost, but softly veiled,

By life's routines and hopes derailed.

Awaken, heart, to the morning's grace,

Let spirit soar, leave no trace,

Faustino Lopez, III

Of doubt or fear that held you tight,

For dawn now breaks the endless night.

In this rebirth, the world is new,

Each breath a chance to seek what's true,

To find the path where soul aligns,

With wonder's call and love's designs.

No longer bound by the mundane,

The spirit's song begins its reign,

Embrace the self you've yet to know,

Let wisdom's light within you grow.

And as the sun climbs ever high,

Touching the earth, caressing the sky,

So too, shall you, in strength and grace,

Find in yourself that sacred place.

The journey starts within the mind,

From Darkness to Light

A quest for truths that few can find,

Yet here, in you, the seed is sown,

To bloom, to thrive, to be fully known.

So rise, and let the dream now fade,

Step into the light that you have made,

For in the dawn, the soul is free,

Awakened to its destiny.

Faustino Lopez, III

Horizons Unseen

In the quiet dawn, where shadows rest,

I walk the path, a soul unpressed,

The earth beneath, my tethered guide,

Yet, in my mind, the heavens glide.

I seek the light beyond the day,

Where stars are born, where dreams convey,

A truth unspoken, yet deeply felt,

In every tear that time has dealt.

For every question left unsaid,

I find a seed in thoughts that thread,

The needle's eye, through torn fabric,

A heart that bleeds, yet feels reborn.

The mountains rise, the valleys bend,

A journey's start with no clear end,

From Darkness to Light

Each step I take, a verse unwritten,

In books of life, my soul is smitten.

But as I climb, with breath in stride,

I find the wind, the world's inside,

A voice that whispers, "Look within,

The path you tread is where you've been."

And so I reach, with hands outstretched,

For knowledge, wisdom, lessons etched,

In stone and sky, in heart and bone,

The universe is mine to own.

Yet, I remain, a humble part,

Of something vast, where journeys start,

A pilgrim's quest, a seeker's dream,

To find the truth in life's grand scheme.

For in each breath, a spark is born,

Faustino Lopez, III

A flame that lights the path forlorn,

I chase the dawn, the night, the sea,

To find the light inside of me.

And though the unknown calls me forth,

I tread with feet upon this earth,

For in each step, a world unfolds,

A journey told, a truth that holds.

So here I stand, on edges bright,

With eyes that pierce the endless night,

Forever drawn to what might be,

In this pursuit, I find my key.

And in the end, when days have passed,

I'll find my soul, my truth at last,

For every step was not in vain,

But part of me, the endless gain.

From Darkness to Light

To grow, to seek, to understand,

To hold the world within my hand,

Yet, know the stars that lie above,

Are not so far from what I love.

For in the quest, I find my home,

In seeking more, I cease to roam,

For all the answers, vast and free,

Reside within the heart of me.

Faustino Lopez, III

Forge of the Moment

In the quiet forge of now, I stand,

A tempered blade in hand,

Crafted by the fire of days past,

Not yet dulled, but sharp as glass.

I walk the line, my pace is steady,

The road is long, the path unready,

Yet every step is carved with care,

Eyes on the prize, but present, aware.

The wind may howl, the skies may roar,

Yet I am anchored, to the core,

In every breath, I find my grace,

In every beat, a steady pace.

The world may push, the world may pull,

But I am neither void nor full,

From Darkness to Light

I stand between the storm and sea,

Where rage has no dominion over me.

For anger's fire, I'll not ignite,

My spirit's flame burns cold and bright,

It fuels the drive, it steels the heart,

To play the game, to play my part.

I'll seize the day with open hands,

Yet, never lose sight of distant lands,

Where freedom waits, where dreams reside,

In balance, both within and wide.

The past is past, the future wide,

But here I stand, here I decide,

With resolute heart and sharpened will,

To climb each mountain, to climb each hill.

In the forge of the moment, I'm made anew,

Faustino Lopez, III

With every choice, with every view,

To live, to strive, to reach the sun,

The journey's long, but far from done.

From Darkness to Light

In the Shadow's Embrace

Beneath the weight of dusk, I stood,

Where shadows stretched and silently grew,

Their whispers brushed my weathered skin,

A tale of change that's overdue.

I once danced in the same old steps,

A ritual carved in ancient stone,

Bound by the rhythm of yesteryears,

Afraid to face the great unknown.

But shadows, they are not to fear,

They know the path we often shun,

They creep within, and softly blend,

Until old patterns come undone.

In the twilight's gentle hold,

I met my shade with quiet grace,

Faustino Lopez, III

We merged as one, and from that bond,

A newer self began to trace.

No longer chained to echoes past,

I shed the skin that once was mine,

Embraced the dark, the light, the all,

A harmony of self entwined.

Now forward steps are bold and sure,

A soul reborn in shadow's hue,

For in the merging, I have found,

A self that's whole, a self that's true.

Inner Sanctum

In the quiet depths where shadows meet,

The heart's true rhythm finds its beat,

Yet we search in distant lands and skies,

For the peace that in ourselves lies.

We weave through days with frantic pace,

Seeking calm in every space,

Yet all the while, within our chest,

A storm churns, unrest, unrest.

How can the world reflect serene,

When our minds are far from clean?

How can peace in others thrive,

When within, we barely survive?

The secret lies in stillness found,

In listening to the inner sound,

Faustino Lopez, III

Where conflicts cease and silence grows,

And every troubled current slows.

To change the world, we must first see,

The war inside, the fractured "we,"

Only when we heal this strife,

Can peace embrace our outer life.

So tend your soul, and calm the sea,

Let inner harmony set you free,

For when the heart knows peace profound,

The world's peace too, will then be found.

From Darkness to Light

Ironclad

I walked a road where shadows bleed,

A path where trust is crushed beneath the heel,

Where promises dissolve like smoke in the night,

And the echoes of false friends are all too real.

Abandoned on the edge of a dream,

With whispers of poison dancing in my veins,

I chased the ghosts of what once was,

But they only led me deeper into pain.

The bottle's comfort was a fleeting embrace,

Its warmth a lie that fed the cold,

And the hunger for escape gnawed at my bones,

But I refused to let the darkness take hold.

Pennies scraped from the bottom of despair,

While debts grew taller than my pride,

Faustino Lopez, III

I fought through the weight of each crushing day,

Knowing no one stood by my side.

Isolation wrapped me in its bitter cloak,

Trust shattered like glass beneath the strain,

But from the shards, I forged my armor,

Ironclad against the world's disdain.

I've known the sting of every cut,

Felt the burn of every scar,

But in the ashes of my wreckage,

I found the steel of who you are.

I no longer seek the hand of false salvation,

No longer yearn for what was never mine,

For in the crucible of my struggle,

I've become the fire, fierce and divine.

Let the past fall away like dead leaves,

From Darkness to Light

Let the broken stay behind the gate,

For I am the master of my own fate,

And not a soul will dictate my fate.

Ironclad, I rise, unbowed,

With every battle, stronger still,

For in the depths of my own making,

I've found the power, the strength, the will.

Faustino Lopez, III

Serene Madness

In the quiet corners of my mind,

Where shadows dance and whisper wind,

A chaos brews, a storm confined,

But here I sit, at peace, aligned.

The world outside, a frantic pace,

Yet, in my head, a tranquil space,

Where thoughts may twist, and fears embrace,

But I remain calm, unchased.

They see the cracks, the fragile thread,

But I've made peace with all that's said.

For in this madness, I am led

To find a calm where others dread.

The highs and lows, they ebb and flow,

But I've learned well to let them go,

From Darkness to Light

To ride the waves, the undertow,

With quiet grace that few will know.

So here I am, a mind askew,

But totally chill, and that's my truth.

In chaos, I've found something new—

A peace that's strong, serene, and true.

Faustino Lopez, III

The Echo of Resistance

In shadows where the quiet lingers,

We build walls to shield the heart,

From thoughts that burn, from wounds that sting,

We fashion armor, part by part.

Yet, in the fortress of our making,

Life's river seeks a way to flow,

But every stone, each rigid wall,

Becomes a dam where sorrows grow.

A thought denied, an emotion spurned,

Turns to echoes in the mind,

A whispered fear, a silent scream,

That no peace or solace finds.

For in the act of pushing back,

We twist the threads of fate too tight,

From Darkness to Light

The more we strain to keep it out,

The more we lose the gift of light.

But if we breathe and let it be,

Embrace the storm, the tear, the flame,

The current softens, winds unwind,

And life returns to us by name.

In yielding, there is strength unknown,

A quiet power, a gentle hand,

To touch the earth, to taste the sky,

And in acceptance, we understand.

That every wave that breaks ashore,

Each cloud that darkens fades, then clears,

Is but a part of nature's song,

A melody that soothes our fears.

So let us dance with what must come,

Faustino Lopez, III

With open hearts and open eyes,

For when we cease to fight the tide,

We find the truth that never dies.

In living all, we lose the pain,

In every breath, we find the gain.

From Darkness to Light

The Gaze of Death

Beneath the sky's eternal shroud,

Where shadows dance and time unspools,

A specter waits, both still and proud,

A guardian of ancient rules.

Death, with eyes like hollow moons,

Gazes deep into our core,

It knows our fears, our whispered tunes,

The secrets we dare not ignore.

Yet, in the face of this dark fate,

We stand with hearts unbroken,

For in our souls, we cultivate,

A strength that needs no token.

We smile back, a quiet grace,

Defiant in our fleeting breath,

Faustino Lopez, III

For life, though brief, is no disgrace,

And so we meet the gaze of Death.

In that exchange, a truth is born,

That life and death are intertwined,

A dance that echoes through the morn,

In rhythms only we can find.

So let the Reaper's grin persist,

For we have learned the art,

To smile back with no resistance,

And keep our peace within the hearts.

From Darkness to Light

The Keeper's Mind

In the quiet chambers of the mind,

Where shadows weave and thoughts unwind,

There lies a garden, wild and vast,

A sanctuary where burdens are cast.

Tend the soil, nurture the seed,

For in its growth lies all we need.

A mind unkempt, a soul unhealed,

Leaves hearts unattended, potential sealed.

We are the keepers, the guardians strong,

Yet, in neglect, our roots go wrong.

How can we guide with wisdom pure,

When our own foundations are insecure?

So pause and breathe, reclaim your peace,

For only then can doubts release.

Faustino Lopez, III

In caring for the self, we find,

The strength to lift the hearts entwined.

For when our own light brightly shines,

It illuminates those left behind.

Intending self, the whole world blooms,

And others rise from their cocoons.

From Darkness to Light

The Quiet of Knowing

In the stillness of the mind's deep well,

Where echoes of doubt fade to a gentle hum,

There lies a truth, too soft for the world's clamor,

A place where we are simply who we are.

Here, in the quiet of knowing,

No shadow looms too large, no storm too fierce,

For we have touched the core of our being,

And in that touch, found a fire that does not burn.

Confidence whispers, not shouts,

It moves like a river, carving paths unseen,

Flowing with the grace of understanding,

Fearless in its dance with possibility.

To know oneself is to hold a secret light,

A beacon that neither flickers nor fades,

Faustino Lopez, III

It shines not for glory, but for truth,

Illuminating the potential within our reach.

In this quiet, we are boundless,

No longer tethered by the chains of fear,

We rise, not to conquer, but to express,

The infinite ways our spirit yearns to create.

And so, we step forward, unafraid,

Not with the roar of certainty,

But with the steady beat of knowing,

That we are enough, and always have been.

From Darkness to Light

The Solitary Sentinel

In the quiet dawn of fractured light,

Where shadows blend with fading night,

A single voice, though soft and clear,

Dares to rise, despite the fear.

The world may turn its gaze away,

And shun the truth, with lips of clay,

But steadfast stand the heart, the soul,

Unyielding in its righteous goal.

For in the midst of silent crowds,

Where whispers weave their darkened shrouds,

There lies a spark, a burning flame,

That knows no shame, that bears no name.

To stand alone, though winds may howl,

And face the storm with furrowed brow,

Faustino Lopez, III

Is to honor justice, pure and true,

To speak for many, though they are few.

So let the doubters scoff and sneer,

Their empty words you need not hear,

For strength is found in those who fight,

To stand for wrong, and stand for right.

And when the night is cold and long,

When echoes fade of distant song,

Remember this, oh, steadfast one,

The battle's end has just begun.

For truth, like light, will always grow,

And in your stand, the world will know,

That courage blooms in solitude,

A solitary sentinel, resolute.

From Darkness to Light

The Tapestry of Us

In the weave of human thread, each strand is unique,

No two alike, in pattern or in hue,

A tapestry of varied voices speaks,

In harmony, the many forms the few.

The dancer's step, the painter's vivid brush,

The quiet thinker, lost in worlds untold,

Each difference, a symphony's soft hush,

Each soul a story, waiting to unfold.

In eyes of blue and brown, in hearts that beat,

In rhythm and in time, yet not the same,

We find our peace in differences we meet,

And celebrate the beauty of each name.

For in the garden of our humankind,

The flowers bloom in colors rich and rare,

Faustino Lopez, III

By cherishing the diverse paths we find,

We cultivate a world beyond compare.

So let us weave our threads with gentle hands,

Embrace the varied tones, the songs we sing,

In unity, our vibrant peace expands,

In every difference, let love take wing.

From Darkness to Light

The Threshold of Unknowing

In the quiet of the night, I stand,

Where certainty fades like grains of sand,

An open mind, a trembling gate,

To let go of all I've called fate.

The echoes of what I've known before,

Release their hold, they cling no more,

Trust in the moment, in the breath,

For wisdom lies beyond what's left.

The stars above, the earth below,

Whisper truths in a gentle flow,

Not in the patterns I've designed,

But in the vastness of an uncharted mind.

Each step forward, a soft surrender,

To the unknown, the great extender,

Faustino Lopez, III

Of consciousness, beyond the frame,

Of names, of forms, of all the same.

To witness is to be set free,

From the chains of past certainty,

For what is seen with eyes anew,

Reveals a world both deep and true.

So here I stand, unbound, aware,

Of a world that's neither here nor there,

An open mind, a boundless shore,

Where the unknown is something more.

From Darkness to Light

The Unyielding

In the shadow of the storm's embrace, I stand,

An oak unbowed, rooted deep in the land.

Winds howl their rage, yet I do not sway,

For my heart is forged in the heat of the fray.

With every lash, the tempest tests my core,

But within, I harbor a strength even more.

Calm as the eye in the hurricane's might,

My resolve shines, a beacon in the night.

They press, they push, with all their might,

But I stand firm, anchored in what is right.

Challenges rise like waves on a shore,

But I am the rock, weathered and sure.

In the face of fire, I do not burn,

In the grip of ice, I do not yearn.

Faustino Lopez, III

For my spirit is steel, my will is flame,

And in the forge of trials, I carve my name.

Let the world roar, let the heavens tear,

I am the constant, the one who dares.

With calm resolve and a heart of stone,

I face the storm, yet remain alone.

For in my soul, a truth does reside,

That strength is quiet, not worn as pride.

I rise each time, no matter the fall,

For I am resilience, unbroken, standing tall.

Thread of Souls

Beneath the stars, we walk alone,

Yet, in our hearts, a truth is known.

A thread unseen, a silken tie,

That binds us all, both low and high.

In laughter shared and tears, we cry,

In silent dreams that pass us by,

We find ourselves in others' gaze,

Reflecting back on our own lost days.

The hand we hold, the words we speak,

Are echoes of the love we seek.

For every heart that beats in time,

Is woven in this web, divine.

So when you feel adrift, apart,

Remember, in the deepest part,

Faustino Lopez, III

We share the breath, we share the soul,

In this grand tapestry, we're whole.

No thread is lost, no thread alone,

For every life, a seed is sown.

And in the weave of time and space,

We find our home, our commonplace.

From Darkness to Light

Threads of Becoming

In the heart of a stubborn truth,

Where shadows guard the ancient way,

We stand as stones, unmoved, uncouth,

Unyielding to the break of day.

The dogma speaks in tongues of steel,

A chain that binds our seeking eyes,

Yet, through the dark, we learn to feel,

The whisper of a soft demise.

The world, a web of woven light,

Each strand a tale of loss and gain,

We grasp the threads with knuckles tight,

Afraid to feel the touch of pain.

But in the grip of doubt, we find,

A spark, a pulse, a tender flame,

Faustino Lopez, III

That burns the veil, frees the mind,

And calls us to our truest name.

We are the roots that twist and blend,

The leaves that kiss the sky above,

The wind that bends, yet does not end,

The quiet force, the act of love.

To confront the walls, the ancient lies,

Is to break and bleed and grow anew,

For in the mirror of our eyes,

The many and the one are true.

So let the stone to dust return,

Let dogma's weight dissolve, unwind,

For in each thread, we live, we learn,

And in the weave, ourselves, we find.

From Darkness to Light

Three Lives Lived

In the first, where dreams took flight,

Bound to my high school's sweetest light,

We wove our plans with threads so fine,

A family's portrait in our mind's design.

But nature's law, unbent, unkind,

Freed my hopes to the silent wind.

A decade's love in silent drift,

As my barren soul began to shift.

The second life, a sullen stream,

Three years as decades, a fevered dream.

A phoenix's dance in reckless flame,

Seared by pleasure, void of aim.

Nights that flickered with transient faces,

Empty echoes in hollow spaces.

Faustino Lopez, III

A wildered heart, lost in its pace,

Sought solace in the frantic chase.

In the third, the dawn's soft glow,

Salvation's hand from depths below.

A renaissance of breath and bloom,

Pulled from the precipice of doom.

The re-married beat of a steady drum,

Crafting a future erstwhile undone.

Life anew, with grace infused,

A spirit once spent, now reclaimed, reused.

Three lives in one, a triptych tale,

Of love, loss, and redemption's grail.

A journey through time's vast expanse,

A triad of chances, a singular dance.

From Darkness to Light

To My Loving Parents

In the gentle hush of dawn's embrace,

To my parents, from a heart's deep space,

Your love, like the ever-flowing tide,

Has carried me, never once did you hide.

In every trial, in laughter and tears,

Your steadfast presence was always near.

Yet time's cruel march, as it winds its way,

Sees me retreat further every day.

Not out of spite nor lack of care,

But a fear that's heavy, dense as air.

Life's cycle spins, its truth I've seen,

Partings, endings, what might have been.

It's not disdain that pulls me afar,

But the dread of losing my guiding star.

Faustino Lopez, III

For in your love, so vast, so true,

I find my strength, my essence, my cue.

Yet, as days grow long and shadows grow deep,

I brace myself for that eternal sleep.

It might seem ungrateful, this wall I build,

But it's love so profound, emotions so filled.

For if fate took you, the pain would be vast,

A devastation, a shadow so cast.

To cushion that blow, I draw away near,

A selfish act, driven by fear.

To preserve my heart, my soul, my song,

In a world without you, where I must be strong.

Know this, dear parents, as life moves on,

My love remains fierce, never withdrawn.

From Darkness to Light

Unveiling the Mirror

In the stillness of night, where shadows fall,

A quiet breath that trembles through the soul,

We glimpse our pain, sharp-edged and small,

And feel the wounds that time cannot console.

The heart, once armored, now opens wide,

A mirror held to every silent tear,

Reflecting grief that cannot hide,

In others' eyes, our own becomes clear.

In knowing sorrow, we find the thread,

That binds our hearts to those in silent cry,

Through suffering's lens, compassion is bred,

A shared humanity, where shadows die.

For in the echo of our deepest ache,

We hear the whispered plea of every soul,

Faustino Lopez, III

And in that knowing, something breaks,

The walls dissolve, and we are whole.

In the mirror of our pain, we find the way,

To walk with others through the darkened night,

For every tear, a guiding ray,

That leads us both towards the light.

From Darkness to Light

Unveiling the Serpent

In shadows cast, I dwelled too long,

A serpent's hiss my only song,

With venom words, it whispered lies,

A puppet to its dark disguise.

Yet deep within, a spark of light,

A voice that beckoned through the night,

To rise, to shed, to stand anew,

To break the chains that once I knew.

The mirror's gaze, a truth untold,

Reflected scars of fear grown old,

But in those lines, I saw a way,

To cast the poison far away.

The hands that held me, now they fall,

No longer bound by shadow's call,

Faustino Lopez, III

I strip the scales of doubt and dread,

And wear the skin of hope instead.

The serpent's coil begins to fade,

Its whispered lies no longer bade,

For in the light, the truth is clear,

The path to freedom, once so near.

I walk it now with steady breath,

Each step is a march away from death,

Towards a dawn of purest air,

Where only light and love can fare.

No more the puppet, no more the pawn,

I greet the world, my fear now gone,

With eyes that see and a heart that knows,

The garden blooms where poison grows.

From Darkness to Light

I cleanse my soul, I rise, I grow,

Through every tear, a seed I sow,

And from the ashes of deceit,

I build a life, a truth replete.

In every shadow, I find light,

A warrior born from the endless night,

And in my heart, a vow is made,

To never fear the darkened blade.

For I am free, the serpent's gone,

I am the dawn, I am the dawn.

Faustino Lopez, III

Unyielding Flame

By shadows cast, I stand unbowed,

No chains of fate can bind me down,

A storm within, fierce and loud,

I carve my path through thorns and crowns.

They whisper doubt in every ear,

But I am fire, wild and free,

No fear to quell, no shame to sear,

In this skin, I choose to be.

The world may twist, may warp, may break,

But I am steel, forged in flame,

Each step I take, each risk I stake,

Is mine alone, with no regret or shame.

They'd have me bend, they'd have me fall,

To fit the mold of their design,

From Darkness to Light

But I rise tall, above it all,

For my truth, I'll never decline.

I walk a road not paved in gold,

But it is mine, rough and true,

With every scar, with very bold,

I wear my strength, and start anew.

Let them talk, let them scorn,

Their words, like dust, will fade away,

For I was born to break the norm,

To live, to fight, to own each day.

So here I stand, unyielding, free,

A soul untamed, a voice unchained,

For all I am, is all I'll be,

Defiant heart, unfeigned, unfeigned.

Faustino Lopez, III

Unyielding Flame -2

In the shadowed hush of night,

Where whispers coil like thorns,

They gather, cloaked in doubt and spite,

To cast their stones, their scorn.

But I stand, a flame unquenched,

My roots deep in the earth,

No storm can break, no wind can bend,

The truth that gave me birth.

Their words, like arrows, sharp and cold,

They aim to pierce my heart,

But each attempt, though fierce and bold,

Falls silent, falls apart.

For I am more than fragile flesh,

am a fire, a spark,

From Darkness to Light

That lights the path through every test,

And brightens every dark.

Let them come with all their might,

Let them sneer and jeer and shout,

For I am strong, I am the light,

That never flickers out.

In their gaze, I see the fear,

The tremor in their eyes,

For they know, no matter near or far,

My spirit will not die.

I rise above, I stand my ground,

Impervious to their disdain,

A force unbowed, a soul unbound,

Unbroken by their pain.

So let them try, and let them fall,

Faustino Lopez, III

For I am built of steel,

A beacon bright, through it all,

Unyielding, strong, and real.

Let the winds howl, let the heavens cry,

Let the world turn against my name,

For I am here, and I'll defy,

Forever an unyielding flame.

From Darkness to Light

Whispers in the Abyss

In the quiet folds of midnight's breath,

I wander through the shadowed veil,

A solitary path I tread, defiant,

As stars blink out and moonlight pales.

Each step a dance on shattered glass,

My mind a whirl of restless fire,

I seek a door, an exit pure,

From echoes of a world that tires.

In opium dreams and fevered light,

I touch the edge of something vast,

A fleeting joy, a sharp delight,

But know too well it cannot last.

The highs are brief, a gilded lie,

A spark before the endless night,

Faustino Lopez, III

Yet in that spark, I glimpse the truth—

A way to flee, a way to fight.

I chase the thrill, the fleeting rush,

As silence swells in hollow rooms,

But every high returns to ash,

And every joy, to whispered gloom.

For solitude, my chosen fate,

To drift where others fear to tread,

In altered states, I find my kin,

A mirror to the thoughts unsaid.

The world outside a distant hum,

My fortress built of quiet pain,

Yet, in the dark, I find a peace,

A solace in the slow refrain.

The journey ends where it began,

From Darkness to Light

Alone, yet somehow more complete,

The highs and lows a distant wave,

As I embrace the final beat.

In solitude, I find my strength,

In echoes of the life I've led,

For all the highs and fleeting joys,

It's in the stillness I am fed.

And so I walk this path alone,

Defiant, with a quiet grace,

For in the end, we all must find,

Our solace in the empty space.

Faustino Lopez, III

Ephemeral Echoes

In the quiet dawn of knowing, we stir,

Awake to the breath of the universe's song,

Whispers of stardust in the sinews of our being,

A dance of atoms, fleeting, yet eternal.

We wander through the corridors of time,

Seeking the shape of our souls in the mirror of the stars,

Transforming in the shadow of our questions,

Chasing the flicker of truth in the depths of the void.

In the grasp of the moment, we find our anchor,

Embracing the pulse of life, fragile and fierce,

The heartbeat of existence echoing through our veins,

A reminder that to live is to be both fleeting and infinite.

Mortality's hand gently rests on our shoulder,

A reminder of the sands slipping through the hourglass,

From Darkness to Light

Yet in that knowing, we find our strength,

The courage to embrace the now, the here, the real.

For in the tension between flesh and spirit,

In the dance between earth and sky,

We discover the grace of being,

The delicate balance of mortality and the eternal.

And as we stand on the edge of understanding,

We see that our place is not a destination,

But a journey, ever-unfolding, ever-becoming,

A quest for meaning that is written in the stars,

Yet, felt in the warmth of the sun on our skin,

In the breath we take, in the moment we live,

We are both the question and the answer,

The fleeting and the forever, the now and the eternal.

Faustino Lopez, III

The Pillar of Solitude

Amidst the silent hum of years,

I stand alone, beneath the weight of time,

Awakened to the bitter truth we share—

A world where shadows cast our forms, unseen.

Yes, it stings, this ancient wound,

Flattery's sweet lies that sour with age,

Generations lulled, then cast aside,

A cruel betrayal written on our bones.

"Stay in line, remain in place," they cry,

"Here, take this scrap, and silence your fire,

Bow your head, and cast your vote for me!"

But no, I shall not feast on hollow gifts,

For hunger fuels the rage that stirs within.

My vision sharpens, and the fog recedes,

And in the company of countless souls,

From Darkness to Light

I find my solitude, my steadfast stand,

A pillar in a world that seeks to break us—

Yes, I stand alone, yet never truly alone.

Faustino Lopez, III

Democracy 2024

In twenty twenty-four, a world unfurled,

Where truths are twisted, lies are hurled,

Misinformation stains the skies,

A shadow cast on open eyes.

In this maze of deceit, we wander lost,

A fragile dream at a perilous cost,

Yet in the heart, a beacon gleams,

Of justice, truth, and human dreams.

To guard democracy's tender flame,

We rise, undaunted, in its name,

For only it can shield our rights,

To privacy in the darkest night.

Civil liberties, our cherished creed,

Demand we act, in thought and deed,

From Darkness to Light

To hold the line, to stand and fight,

For basic human rights, our guiding light.

Against the storm of false pretense,

We seek the truth, in its defense,

In every heart, a steadfast plea,

To protect our shared democracy.

Faustino Lopez, III

The Art of Release

In the quiet dusk of fading days,

Where shadows linger, and memories haze,

We clutch the echoes of what once was near,

Bound by the past, by loss, by fear.

Yet, to find the joy that life bestows,

We must unbind what the heart still knows.

Let go of echoes that softly fade,

And bless the lessons that time has made.

For in the ashes of what is lost,

Rests the warmth of love's true cost.

Be grateful for the embers that stay,

Guiding our path to the light of day.

Look forward now, with eyes unclouded,

Past the ruins where dreams once crowded.

From Darkness to Light

For in the dawn of what is yet to be,

Lies the promise of a soul set free.

So release the grip on yesteryear,

Embrace what's left, hold it dear.

And with open arms, welcome what's next,

For in letting go, we are truly blessed.

Faustino Lopez, III

The Churn

In the rush, I find my solace,

A blur of tasks, a ceaseless hum,

I tether myself to the grindstone's call,

For if I stop, the silence comes.

The quiet, a void, too vast, too deep,

Where echoes of the past reside,

So I spin the wheel, I stir the pot,

And keep the ghosts at bay inside.

Each step I take is a measured dance,

To a rhythm that numbs the ache,

The fear of pause, a yawning chasm,

Where old wounds threaten to awake.

I built my tower of busy hands,

Each brick a task, each stone a goal,

From Darkness to Light

And climbed it high, beyond the clouds,

To flee the truths I dare not know.

Yet in the heights, the air grows thin,

The cost of breath a heavy toll,

The feelings locked, the tears unshed,

Weigh down my weary, guarded soul.

I've carved success from frantic days,

A monument to my control,

But beneath the gleaming surface lies

A heart that bears a hidden hole.

The churn, my friend, my fierce escape,

Has led me far, but now I see,

That in the race, I've lost the parts

Of who I was, of who I'd be.

Now standing still, I face the truth,

Faustino Lopez, III

The pace I set, a shield of glass,

And as it cracks, the echoes rise,

The past I fled begins to pass.

But here, amidst the ruin's dust,

I find a seed of something new,

A space to breathe, to mourn, to heal,

And let the light of dawn break through.

From Darkness to Light

Beacon Within

In shadows deep, where fears reside,

A flicker stirs, but tries to hide.

The world outside, so cold and vast,

Yet inward still, you hold the mast.

No guiding star, no northern gleam,

But in your soul, a buried beam.

It waits for you, to lift it high,

To cast your own light through the sky.

The darkest nights may claw and tear,

But in that fight, you find your flare.

No need for moons to mark your way,

You are the dawn, you are the day.

So let the tempest roar and rage,

For you, my friend, will turn the page.

Faustino Lopez, III

A fire within, so fierce, so bright—

Be your own light to face your night.

From Darkness to Light

Echoes of Grace

Whisper softly, tender heart,

In the stillness of your mind,

Where shadows linger, fears depart,

Let gentleness be what you find.

Speak with warmth, a soothing balm,

To the wounds the world can't see,

In your voice, a sacred calm,

A refuge where you can be free.

Breathe in words like morning light,

That touch the soul, that heal the night,

For you are worthy, pure and bright,

A beacon in the darkest fight.

Hold yourself with tender hands,

Like the fragile, precious soul you are,

Faustino Lopez, III

In this moment, understand,

Your worth is written in the stars.

So, talk to you with love and care,

With the grace, you'd give another,

For in your heart, beyond compare,

Lives a strength like no other.

Each word you speak, each thought you hold,

Let it be gentle, let it be kind,

In this embrace, let love unfold,

For you, dear soul, are truly divine.

From Darkness to Light

In Defiance of the Dark

Better to fight and fall, I say,

Then, live a life that bleeds to gray,

For hope is forged in battles lost,

In scars that tell of courage tossed.

I'll face the tempest, break the tide,

With dreams that burn but will not hide,

A heart that stumbles, fierce and wild,

An orphan thought, a reckless child.

Let shadows whisper, doubt and sneer,

I'll meet their darkness without fear,

For every wound that sears my skin,

Will light a fire that grows within.

And if I fall, then let it be,

A blaze that sets the midnight free,

Faustino Lopez, III

For better to burn in hope's cruel flame,

Then, die untouched with a whispered name.

From Darkness to Light

My Legacy

In the quiet heart of service, beneath the public's sight,

A choice was made, not for gold or fame's bright light.

A path less trodden, where compassion's seeds are sown,

To stand by souls forgotten, in shadows cast, alone.

These are the lives, frayed at the edges, worn and torn,

Bridges to the past in flames, relations sworn.

Yet, in this realm of constant trials and silent pleas,

A beacon shines, to mend these tattered tapestries.

Belief in self, a fragile thread, so hard to weave,

Through eyes that have seen despair, yet dare to dream.

To instill hope, a Herculean task, against the tide,

Where every small victory is a monumental stride.

Day by day, a struggle, under watchful skies so vast,

Hoping to make a difference, in futures not yet cast.

The reward is not in riches but in whispers of renewal,

As those once lost find paths to redemption, beautiful.

Faustino Lopez, III

Remember, the journey of recovery is endless, steep,

A road marred with setbacks, a hill so very steep.

Yet, with each fall, a lesson in resilience, a grace,

A testament to the strength within, a better place.

For in this fight, not just the fallen, but we, too, grow,

Learning the power of patience and hope's gentle glow.

The true measure of success is not in the falls but in the rise,

A testament to the human spirit under the vast, open skies.

So let us walk this path with empathy as our guide,

Helping others to find their way, with strides taken in stride.

For nothing is more fulfilling than to see a life reborn,

In the quiet heart of service, where true heroes are sworn.

About The Author

Faustino Lopez, III, has dedicated nearly thirty years of his life to serving as a Community Supervision Officer, rising to the position of Director within his department. His career brought him face-to-face with the complexities of human behavior, exposing him to the often-overlooked emotional toll of vicarious trauma. This role, while deeply fulfilling, also led him on a personal journey through the dark valleys of the mind, where the weight of his experiences nearly led him to self-destruction.

In "From Darkness to Light: The Memoirs of a Healing Mind," Tino chronicles his transformative journey from despair to understanding, exploring how the challenges he faced both professionally and personally became the catalysts for his growth. Through vulnerability and self-reflection, he found a way to embrace the darkness within, discovering resilience and healing.

Now, with his memoir, Tino hopes to extend a hand to others who find themselves lost in the shadows, offering them the insight and hope needed to rediscover the light.